OAK TREE TALES

Miss Mouse

Dorothea King

Winter was over. Deep in the middle of the forest where the huge oak tree stood the first primroses opened their yellow petals in the warm sunshine and everyone knew Spring had come.

As the sunshine swept slowly over the huge tree, a tiny window in the bottom of the trunk was thrown open and a little mouse popped her head out to sniff the morning air.

"What a lovely day," she said to herself.

"Indeed it is," answered a voice from above.

Quite soon, a fine red squirrel appeared outside her window. He was dressed in a green chequered coat, cream trousers and carried a silver-topped cane. Miss Mouse thought he looked most elegant.

"Off for your morning walk, Sir Squirrel?" she asked politely.

"Yes indeed," he replied, and took a deep breath of Spring air. "A brisk ten minute walk and I shall be ready for a day's work."

"Well, I mustn't keep you chatting," said Miss Mouse. "Have a lovely time."

Once the squirrel had gone on his way, she decided to start her Spring-cleaning.

First she took down her curtains, then she removed the cover from her thistledown quilt and finally went round the house collecting all the cushion covers.

She piled everything into a big tub of hot soapy water and proceeded to wash the lot.

Singing gaily to herself she rubbed, scrubbed and rinsed until her linen basket was full.

On her way to the washing line she met Mistress Hedgehog who, like Miss Mouse, had been doing her Spring cleaning. She was about to hang her washing on the line.

Mistress Hedgehog lived in a little house under a pile of dry leaves at the bottom of the tree. It was a warm cosy house built in among the roots and surrounded by soft green moss.

"Morning, Mistress Hedgehog," said the mouse politely.

"And a fine one it is to be sure," came the reply.

They chatted as they hung up their washing and afterwards the hedgehog invited Miss Mouse in for coffee and a cream cake. Unfortunately, Miss Mouse had never been able to entertain the hedgehog in her house for it was much too small, but occasionally in the Summer she would spread a large cloth over the toadstool in the clearing and invite Mistress Hedgehog to tea.

Quite soon they were sipping coffee from Mistress
Hedgehog's finest bone china cups and were about to
start on the cream cakes when there was a loud rat-a-tat-
tat on the door. A frantic voice yelled out, "Mistress
Hedgehog! Mistress Hedgehog! Come quickly!"

The hedgehog put down her cup in disgust. "It's that stupid rabbit," she said to the mouse. "Now what's he up to? Another one of his pranks, I'll be bound."

Master Rabbit lived quite close to Mistress Hedgehog, in fact one of his burrows went right under her house.

He was a bit of a nuisance and she was always having to complain about the amount of dirt he made on her front doorstep. The hedgehog opened the door.

The rabbit took a deep breath and pointed to the door. "The moon's falling out of the sky!" he said breathlessly.

The mouse and the hedgehog looked at each other in disgust.

"Don't be ridiculous," snapped Mistress Hedghog.

"If you don't believe me come and see for yourself."

When they were all out in the clearing the rabbit pointed a shaking paw at the sky. "There it is...see!"

And indeed he was right, for just above the top of the trees was a large, round, yellow object with a smiling face.

"Well, bless my soul!" said Mistress Hedgehog in astonishment.

All three of them gazed open-mouthed at the yellow object which floated gracefully above them and seemed to be getting lower and lower. As they stood there absolutely speechless, Sir Squirrel came rushing into the clearing.

"Have you seen it?" he gasped.

Nobody replied; they were still speechless.

"What do you think it is, old man?" said the squirrel to the rabbit.

"The moon of course," replied the rabbit in a daze.

"The moon! That's stupid. If the moon fell out of the sky, we'd all be smashed to smithereens."

"All right, Mr. Know-it-all, what do you think it is?" snapped the hedgehog who hadn't much time for the squirrel.

"I really don't know, but it definitely isn't the moon...in fact, in spite of my vast experience, I really don't know what it is."

The moon by this time was directly overhead and still seemed to be getting lower.

"If we follow it we might find out," suggested the rabbit.

Everyone thought this was a good idea.

"I'll just get my shawl," said Miss Mouse. "Don't go without me."

When she returned, the others were all hopping up and down in excitement.

"It's getting lower!" squealed the hedgehog.

"By jove, it is as well!" replied the squirrel.

"If it does we'll all be killed," announced the rabbit.

"Come on, my dears, it's nearly out of sight," yelled the squirrel, and dashed off down a woodland path in the direction the moon was travelling.

As they all ran along the path they caught sight of the yellow object between the trees getting lower...and lower...and lower.

By the time they caught up it was suspended from a branch only a few feet off the ground, smiling down at them. They all stood in a little huddle puffing and panting from their mad dash through the wood, gazing up at the smiling face.

"Do you think we should say hello?" whispered Miss Mouse.

"Don't quite know what we should do in a situation like this," pondered Sir Squirrel. "He's still quite a long way up. He might not hear us."

As they stood wondering what to do or say, a sudden gust of wind swept through the clearing and carried the moon down...and down...until it was inches above the ground.

"Oh...!" they all gasped together.

It was then that Miss Mouse noticed a curious thing. From underneath the moon hung a piece of string. Quickly she darted forward and, before the others could stop her, had grabbed the end which was trailing on the ground.

"Look!" she yelled excitedly, and held up the string for the others to see.

They all rushed forward but before they got to her a terrible thing happened. Another gust of wind suddenly tossed the moon high in the air and Miss Mouse was yanked off her feet. Within seconds she was floating steadily upwards.

"Oh..hh.hh!" she cried. "Help me...help!!" But it was too late...she was rising fast.

The others ran round in circles bumping into one another as they watched Miss Mouse getting smaller and smaller as she rose higher and higher into the sky. Finally, she disappeared over the tops of the trees and out of sight.

"Remarkable!" said the squirrel.

"What a take-off!" said the rabbit.

"My friend's gone for ever," sobbed the hedgehog, and flung herself at the squirrel, sobbing uncontrollably.

"Steady on, my dear," he said, and gently pushed her away to wipe the tears off his jacket.

"Well, what do we do now?" asked the rabbit.

They all looked at one another, each waiting for the other to come up with a solution. At last Sir Squirrel suggested they all go back to his place to have a glass of oakapple wine to steady their nerves. As nobody else could think of a better idea, that is exactly what they did.

All this time, Miss Mouse had been floating along, clinging to the piece of string and yelling with all her might.

She had been travelling in a southerly direction for about twenty minutes when she was joined by a flock of starlings who were most curious about her method of flying.

"Migrating, are you?" asked one.

"Don't be stupid," replied Miss Mouse. "Any fool can see I'm hanging onto the moon."

"I always thought the moon was made of cheese," remarked an elderly bird called Alf.

His friend, who was flying alongside, became quite excited by this remark. "Cheese," he yelled. "Well, in that case I'll go and have a peck...most partial to a bit of cheese I am." And with that he zoomed upwards.

Within seconds there was
an enormous...BANG! and
the next minute, Miss Mouse
found herself falling out of
the sky.

   Hurtling toward the tree
tops at an alarming rate and
gathering speed, she fell...
down...down...down and
then...BUMP!
   She had miraculously
landed in the topmost branches
of a large pine tree.

She was still sitting there,
feeling dazed and bewildered,
when she was startled by
the sound of a voice.
   "Dropped in for lunch,
have you?"
   Miss Mouse couldn't see
from where the voice had come.

   Suddenly the air around
her was filled with the
delicious aroma of
beefburger and chips, and
her whiskers began to
quiver.

Quickly, she scurried towards the trunk of the tree which was where the smell seemed to be coming from and there, hidden behind a pine branch, was a round window. Miss Mouse tip-toed forward to peer inside and saw to her amazement a little old lady cooking over a large old-fashioned stove.

Although the old lady didn't look up she seemed to know Miss Mouse was there. "Come inside, my dear...you'll find the door a bit further around the trunk."

Miss Mouse stuttered, "Th...Thank you," and carefully walked round the tree until she found a small door. It was painted green to match the pine and had a moon-shape carved in the wood. Miss Mouse gently turned the brass door knob and went inside.

The door led into a hall which had a mat with WELCOME written on it, a hat-stand with a funny pointed hat hanging from it, and a broomstick stood in the corner. She stood in the hall until the old lady called, "Don't be shy, I've been expecting you."

The old lady was putting two plates of steaming food on the table which was already set for two.

"Sit yourself down, my dear," she said. "Don't let it get cold, chips are awful when they're cold...don't you agree?"

Miss Mouse nodded in astonishment and sat herself down at the table.

"I'll just chop Midnight's food up and then I'll join you...he does love his lunch, don't you, Puss?"

A large, black, fluffy cat with a smily face left his basket by the fire and purred around the old lady's legs. Once he was busy eating she bustled over to the table and sat herself down opposite Miss Mouse who hadn't taken a single bite of her food.

"Eat up, child," she said. "After a shock like you've had this morning you must be starving."

The old lady took a big bite of the juicy beefburger. "Delicious," she declared.

Miss Mouse couldn't contain herself any longer. "How do you know about this morning, and how did you know I was coming?" she asked.

The old lady put down her knife and fork and giggled, her eyes twinkling with mischief. "Bless my soul, child, haven't you guessed? I'm a witch! They call me Witch White."

Miss Mouse was almost paralysed with fright.

"A w..witch!" she stuttered. "But..w..witches are wicked."

The little old lady began to laugh again. "And I expect you've heard we cast wicked spells and boil bats' tongues and things," she giggled.

"Well, yes." admitted Miss Mouse.

"Load of nonsense," chuckled Witch White. "For one thing, you can't buy bats' tongues anymore, and for another the silly rumour about witches all started years ago...so long, in fact, that nobody can remember how it started. Now eat your lunch and then we must see about getting you home."

Miss Mouse did as she was told and ate every bit on her plate...and then had a double portion of chocolate ice cream to follow.

All through lunch, the old lady told Miss Mouse stories about woodland creatures and fairy folk. Before they realised it, the afternoon had flown by and it was nearly tea-time.

"My goodness me, look at the time... I really must get you home."

"How will you do that?" enquired Miss Mouse.

"Why, fly of course," laughed Witch White. I'll just get my broomstick."

"Oh, no thank you... I've had quite enough of flying for one day," said Miss Mouse.

"How silly of me, of course you have," replied the old lady. "Now how can I...? Ah, I've got it. How would you like to travel by fairy coach?"

"Oh yes," said Miss Mouse, clapping her hands together. "That would be splendid."

"Well, you just come with me," said Witch White and put her witch's hat on.

Miss Mouse followed her down a long, long staircase which wound its way round the tall tree until eventually they were on the ground.

The old lady hurried along a little path with Miss Mouse following and soon they came to a mossy bank.
In among the primroses and bluebells there were lots of little brightly painted doors.

"Cooeee," the old lady called softly and to Miss Mouse's amazement all the little doors flew open and out came dozens of little fairies. How pleased they were to see the old lady.

Miss Mouse was introduced to all of them and then the old lady explained why they had come. The fairies were only too delighted to loan Miss Mouse their coach and within minutes she was stepping into the most perfect little coach she had ever seen, drawn by four miniature white horses. How grand she felt.

The old lady kissed her goodbye and made her promise to visit again soon, and with that the four little horses trotted off into the forest.

Miss Mouse sat back enjoying the ride, she didn't have to guide the horses for they seemed to know exactly which path to take.

On they went past elfin villages, through fields of bracken, along mossy paths until eventually they reached the big oak tree and Miss Mouse was home.

By this time the sun had set and the first stars were beginning to twinkle in the sky.

Miss Mouse alighted, very grandly from the coach and with her nose in the air walked past the hedgehog, the squirrel and the rabbit who stood open-mouthed in astonishment. Not one of them said a word.

As Miss Mouse reached her own front door, she turned round and said, "I shall tell you all about it in the morning." And with that she went in and shut the door behind her.

While she was getting ready for bed she thought about the big yellow object and wondered what it was, but quite soon she was snuggling down into her little bed and sound asleep.

Well into the night the moon looked in through her window and smiled down as if to say "I know what it was..."

Do you?